Dear Parents,

Welcome to the Scholastic Reader series. We have taken over 80 years of experience with teachers, parents, and children and put it into a program that is designed to match your child's interests and skills.

Level 1— Short sentences and stories made up of words kids can sound out using their phonics skills, and words that are important to remember.

Level 2— Longer sentences and stories with words kids need to know, and new "big" words that they will want to know.

Level 3— From sentences to paragraphs to longer stories, these books have large "chunks" of texts and are made up of a rich vocabulary.

Level 4— First chapter books with more words and fewer pictures.

It is important that children learn to read well enough to succeed in school and beyond. Here are ideas for reading this book with your child:

- Look at the book together. Encourage your child to read the title and make a prediction about the story.
- Read the book together. Encourage your child to sound out words when appropriate. When your child struggles, you can help by providing the word.
- Encourage your child to retell the story. This is a great way to check for comprehension.
- Have your child take the fluency test on the last page to check progress.

Scholastic Readers are designed to support your child's efforts to learn how to read at every age and every stage. Enjoy helping your child learn to read and love to read.

— **Francie Alexander**
Chief Education Officer
Scholastic Education

No part of this publication may be reproduced, or stored in a retrieval system, or transmitted in any form or by any means, electronic, mechanical, photocopying, recording, or otherwise, without written permission of the publisher. For information regarding permission, write to Scholastic Inc., Attention: Permissions Department, 557 Broadway, New York, NY 10012.

Copyright © 2004 by Hans Wilhelm.

Activities copyright © 2004 Scholastic Inc.
All rights reserved. Published by Scholastic Inc.
SCHOLASTIC, CARTWHEEL BOOKS, and associated logos
are trademarks and/or registered trademarks of Scholastic Inc.

Library of Congress Cataloging-in-Publication Data is available.

ISBN: 0-439-68264-9

12 11 10 9 8 7 6 5 4 3 2 1   4 5 6 7 8 9/0
Printed in the U.S.A.   23
First printing, November 2004

I HATE BEDTIME!

by Hans Wilhelm

Scholastic Reader — Level 1

SCHOLASTIC INC.

New York   Toronto   London   Auckland   Sydney
Mexico City   New Delhi   Hong Kong   Buenos Aires

I'm not tired.

I hate bedtime.

I will stay up and play.

It's too dark
to go outside.

I'll play with Cat.

Cat is sleeping.

Baby is sleeping, too.

Everyone is sleeping.

I have an idea!

Here's a slipper.

Let's go!

Whee!
What fun!

Oh, no!

Crash!

I'm very sleepy now.